At the Edge of the Woods

A Counting Book

Cynthia Cotten

illustrated by Reg Cartwright

Henry Holt and Company ◆ New York

Henry Holt and Company, LLC, Publishers since 1866
115 West 18th Street, New York, New York 10011
www.henryholt.com

Henry Holt is a registered trademark of Henry Holt and Company, LLC
Text copyright © 2002 by Cynthia Cotten
Illustrations copyright © 2002 by Reg Cartwright
All rights reserved.
Distributed in Canada by H. B. Fenn and Company Ltd.

Library of Congress Cataloging-in-Publication Data
Cotten, Cynthia.
At the edge of the woods: a counting book / Cynthia Cotten; illustrated by Reg Cartwright.
Summary: A variety of animals, birds, and insects enjoy the flowers
and trees of the forest early one morning.
[1. Forests and forestry—Fiction. 2. Forest animals—Fiction.
3. Forest plants—Fiction. 4. Stories in rhyme.] I. Cartwright, Reg, ill. II. Title.
PZ8.3.C8284 At 2002   [E]—dc21   2001005205

ISBN 0-8050-6354-4 / First Edition—2002
Printed in the United States of America on acid-free paper. ∞
1 3 5 7 9 10 8 6 4 2

For my family: Steven, Amanda, and Christopher, with love
—C. C.

For Lydia
—R. C.

At the edge of the woods, the grass grows tall,
the daisies dance, and the blackbirds call.

One chipmunk lives in the old stone wall
at the edge of the deep, dark woods.

At the edge of the woods, the treetops sway.
The sunrise brings a brand-new day.

TWO spotted fawns come out to play
at the edge of the deep, dark woods.

2

At the edge of the woods, a pond lies still
in the misty early morning chill.

Three furry foxes drink their fill
at the edge of the deep, dark woods.

At the edge of the woods, the sun's warm rays
clear away the morning haze.

Four little lizards lounge and laze
at the edge of the deep, dark woods.

4

At the edge of the woods, the breezes blow,
buttercups and clovers grow.

Five buzzy bees zoom to and fro
at the edge of the deep, dark woods.

5

6

At the edge of the woods, in the summer heat,
blackberries ripen, warm and sweet.

Six sassy blue jays love to eat
at the edge of the deep, dark woods.

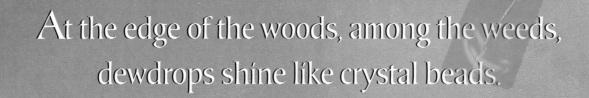

At the edge of the woods, among the weeds,
dewdrops shine like crystal beads.

Seven sleek field mice gather seeds
at the edge of the deep, dark woods.

At the edge of the woods, a twisty vine
tangles itself in a deep green pine.

Eight speckled sparrows perch in a line
at the edge of the deep, dark woods.

8

At the edge of the woods, by the apple tree,
grow Queen Anne's lace and chicory.

Nine bright butterflies flutter free
at the edge of the deep, dark woods.

9

At the edge of the woods, there is an arch
made by the roots of a lacy larch.

Ten tiny ants are on the march
at the edge of the deep, dark woods.

At the edge of the woods, a big burly bear
lumbers out of his cozy lair

into the meadow to get some air

and . . .

ten ants,

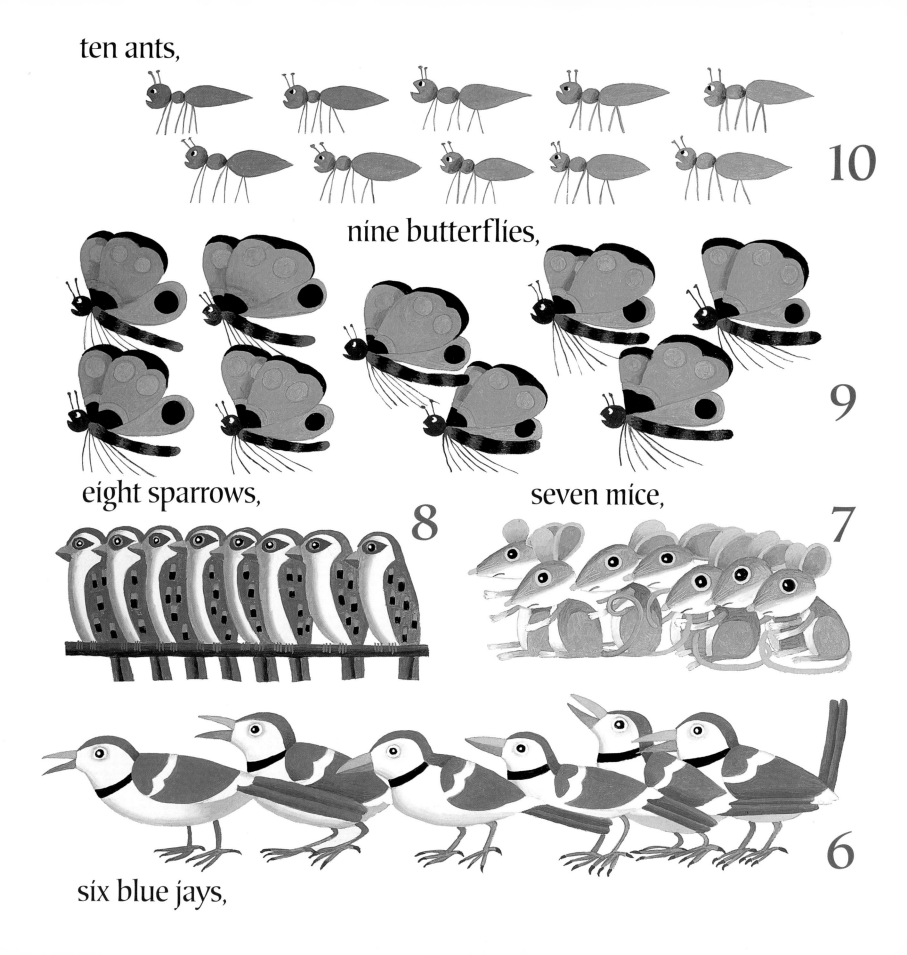

10

nine butterflies,

9

eight sparrows,

8

seven mice,

7

six blue jays,

6

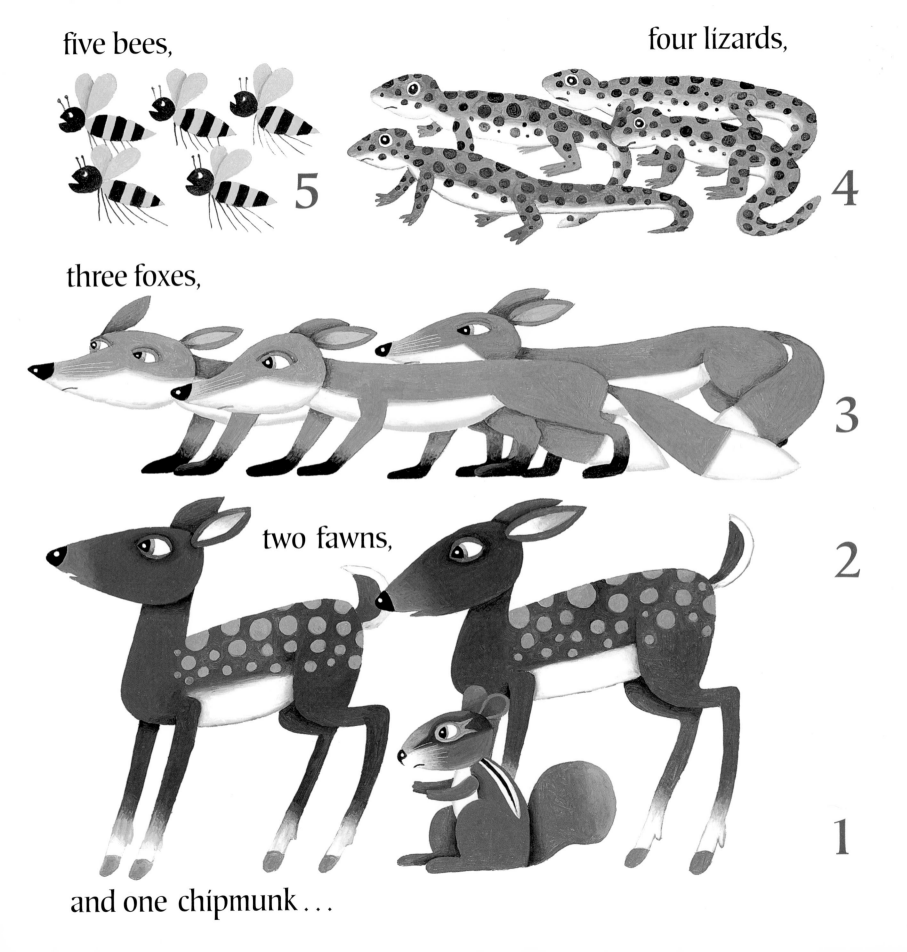

five bees, 5

four lizards, 4

three foxes, 3

two fawns, 2

1

and one chipmunk …

. . . Hide

at the edge of the deep, dark woods.